THE BLUE ORNAMENT

G. SCOTT SPARROW

Also by G. Scott Sparrow

Lucid Dreaming: Dawning of the Clear Light (A.R.E.)

I Am With You Always: True Stories of Encounters with Jesus (Bantam)

Blessed Among Women: Encounters with Mary and Her Message (Crown)

Sacred Encounters with Jesus (Ave Maria)

Sacred Encounters with Mary (Ave Maria)

Healing the Fisher King: A Flyfisher's Grail Quest (BlueMantle)

THE BLUE ORNAMENT

G. SCOTT SPARROW

BlueMantle
United States of America

BlueMantle Press
www.bluemantle.net
E-mail: info@bluemantle.net

Library of Congress Control Number: 2005931769

Printed in the United States

Cover photos and design by G. Scott Sparrow
The Blue Ornament/ by G. Scott Sparrow

ISBN: 978-0-9665485-6-3

BODY, MIND & SPIRIT / Inspiration & Personal Growth / OCC019000

JUVENILE FICTION / Holidays & Celebrations / Christmas / JUV017010

RELIGION / Holidays / Christmas / REL034020

First Printing January, 2015

Table of Contents

One: A Perfect Stranger 1

Two: The Mysterious Ornament 13

Three: What Fathers Long For 23

Four: What Mothers Seek 37

Five: What Children Dream Of 47

Six: What Only Brothers Can Give 55

Seven: What Andrew Found 69

Eight: What Little Beasts Need 77

Nine: The Stranger Returns 83

For Ryan

Chapter One
A Perfect Stranger

Andrew realized that he was probably dreaming as he flew above the two oak trees that marked the entrance to his neighborhood, but he tried not to think about it. He loved to fly in his dreams, and he didn't want to wake up too soon. He flew with his arms outstretched toward the rising sun until he reached the left curve in the road that took him deeper into Old Comfort, a neighborhood full of winding roads and thick pine woods beside the bay. Just before he reached Dogwood Lane, he took a shortcut over the Evans' house, and came down lower and circled his home.

There, below, he saw his stepfather Cyrus walking his dog Penny in the front yard. Andrew floated over the house and saw his mom bundled up in a blanket, drinking her morning coffee on the patio. A book lay open in her lap, as she watched two rabbits playing on the dew-covered grass near the edge of the woods.

Turning away from the house, Andrew flew higher and saw the sun climbing over the pine trees that lined the bay. Then, strangely, the sun grew larger and larger until a bright whitish golden circle filled the entire sky. And then it seemed to fill his whole body with a feeling of deep happiness. Moments later he awakened in his bed at his dad's house with sunlight pouring into the room.

He laid in bed awhile, enjoying the warmth of the sunlight on his face and relishing the memory of his dream. But thoughts of the dream quickly faded as the smell of oatmeal and fresh muffins floated up from the kitchen. He knew that his stepmom Mary would soon be calling him for breakfast so he slowly rolled out of bed and slipped into his jeans.

Stepping carefully over the herd of dinosaurs that huddled together on the floor, Andrew looked down and saw that his new baby stegosaurus was lying on its side. Andrew frowned and muttered, "He's been here again, that miserable cat!"

Andrew dropped to the floor and reached under his bed, uncovering his secret weapon—a super squirter water gun. He scrambled into position, holding the gun to his shoulder, and jumped out into the hallway.

"Where are you, you mangy cat!?"

Creeping down the hallway with his gun poised for action, Andrew kept a sharp eye out for Diggory. He reached the far end of the hallway and saw the cat's tail peeking out from under a chair. "I gotcha!" he whispered. He took a deep breath and prepared to squeeze off a shot that would wipe Diggory from the face of the earth, or at least make him think twice about messing up Andrew's room.

"Andrew, come down for breakfast. We have to get to the store soon," Mary called up from the kitchen.

Andrew let the gun fall to his side, his shoulders slumping in disappointment. "Yes, ma'am."

Returning to his room, he put the gun back under his bed after carefully wrapping it in a towel. He knew that Mary and his dad expected him to keep it in the garage.

After Andrew pulled a sweatshirt over his head, he paused to look out the window. To the north, the tops of the tall pines rose above the houses. He could see almost all the way to his mom's house, a mile away, where he lived most of the time and where the towering pines surrounded his home. He gazed across the distance, wishing that he really could fly from one house to the other and tie them together with the red ribbon that lay on the floor.

Three years had gone by since that day when his mom had been reading to Andrew on the sofa in the den. His dad had come in and said something that made her cry. Andrew cried, too, because he knew somehow that everything he'd known and loved would be changing, even though he didn't understand why. His dad left that day and never came back home.

Things were better now, and the only thing that remained of that unpleasant time was a deep sadness that would sometimes creep over Andrew when he got into bed at night. When it did, he would usually cry himself to sleep and wake up feeling better the next day. It was a big step when he finally admitted to his dad that sometimes he wished that his father lived farther away, because it hurt so much to have him so close, but not back at home. Instead of getting mad at Andrew, his dad just hugged him and thanked him for talking about his feelings.

In spite of his sadness, Andrew was relieved that his parents seemed happier now. He loved his stepfather, who was as good to him as anyone had ever been. Cyrus was a vegetarian, though, and he would sometimes look ill when Andrew forgot and went on and on about how the meat-eating dinosaurs would devour their plant-eating neighbors.

Andrew's dad seemed happier since he'd met Mary. There was something mysterious about his stepmom, as if she knew something that she was not saying. Mary would often sit with Andrew on the sofa, listening to him talk. He would always feel better, even though sometimes she said very little. She would nod and smile as Andrew talked, and sometimes she would close her eyes looking very peaceful. His dad often said that Mary had a gift that was especially rare—she listened carefully to what people said.

While Andrew and his mom remained as close as ever, he couldn't talk to her as easily about what had happened, because she would get upset and have to go in the other room.

But this morning, thoughts of the past faded away, much like the fog did when the sun rose. Andrew was excited, because this Christmas promised to be the very best one he'd ever had. Gram was coming to spend Christmas at his mom's. And Mary's children—Tommy and Sarah—would be coming in a couple of days from Georgia to spend the holidays with his dad and Mary. Andrew would be going back and forth between his mom's and dad's, and lots of things had been planned.

As he finished dressing, Andrew looked around his room. He decided that there was definitely room for a few more dinosaurs. He figured that between his parents, his aunts and uncles, and his grandparents, he would receive all the dinosaurs that he wanted—the T-Rex, the raptor, and the triceratops—and a lot more, too, that he hadn't asked for. He could hardly wait for Christmas morning when he'd finally get to open all of his presents at both houses. With that thought, he hurried down the stairs for breakfast.

Stephen MacClean was standing by the window sipping a cup of coffee when Andrew entered the kitchen.

"Morning, Dad," Andrew said as he slipped into his chair at the table.

"Morning." Stephen took his seat at the head of the table. "Are you ready for Christmas?" he asked with a smile.

Andrew shrugged and said, "Sure. I'm always ready to open presents."

Stephen frowned. "What about the others? Have you made your shopping list?"

"Oh, that." Andrew set his orange juice down with a thump. "I thought you were just joking."

"No, I wasn't." Stephen glanced at Mary as she came back into the kitchen carrying a pad and pencil. "You need to learn how to enjoy giving to others."

"But I was saving my money to buy something that I might not get for Christmas."

"You need to think about someone besides yourself, young man," Stephen said firmly.

"It's not fair...I can't buy presents for everyone with only $12. That's all I've saved!"

"Andrew," Mary interrupted, placing her hand on Andrew's. "We told you we'd match what you were able to save. So you'll actually have $24 to work with. I think you can manage with that," she said encouragingly.

"I don't know what to get Tommy and Sarah," Andrew complained. "I hardly know them." He thought that might get him out of the task.

"Well, you can ask them when they arrive." Mary rose and went to the stove, returning to the table carrying two bowls of oatmeal, setting one in front of him. "Eat up."

"It isn't fair," Andrew muttered.

Stephen sighed and walked to the refrigerator, taking a letter and a photo of a dark haired boy out from under a magnet.

"Do you remember Mario?" Stephen asked, as he returned to the table.

Andrew shrugged. "Sort of. He's that kid in Mexico you send money to."

"Right, we sponsor him." Stephen adjusted his glasses. "Let me read you something." He scanned the letter. "Here it is."

Stephen read, "I want to thank you for my Christmas money. This year after buying a pair of shoes for school, I will give what remains to my mother and father so they can buy school books for my brothers and sisters."

Andrew looked shocked. "He has to buy his own shoes!?"

Stephen nodded. "And he doesn't mention any toys either." Stephen glanced at Mary. "This is the last time we'll discuss this. I think you know what we expect of you."

Silence fell around the table, as Andrew thought about having to buy gifts for everyone in his family. In fact, it was about the only thing he thought about for the rest of the day. Finally, he went to bed with no idea how he was going to do what his dad and Mary required of him.

That night, after being asleep for only a couple of hours, Andrew awakened to a sound. He sat up in his bed to listen. At first he thought that it must have been Diggory knocking the Christmas balls off the tree again. But then he heard what sounded like someone singing a song. Andrew knew that the front and back doors were locked, and that there wasn't supposed to be anyone else in the house.

Yet, for some odd reason, Andrew wasn't afraid. He got out of bed, tiptoed past the closed door to his dad's room, and looked down the stairs into the front hall. A light was coming from the den, lighting up the hallway with a warm glow.

"Dad must have forgotten to unplug the tree lights," Andrew concluded. "I'll go do it myself." Thinking that he only imagined hearing a voice, Andrew headed down the stairs. Maybe, he thought, he could investigate the lumpy package that Mary had wrapped for him earlier that day. It was shaped just like the triceratops that he wanted. And maybe one of the horns would "accidentally" poke through the wrapping paper.

As Andrew walked from the front hall toward the den, he heard the voice again. Someone was definitely humming! It was then that Andrew noticed that other things seemed strange. Both doors to his father's office were open, and the angel merry-go-round had been set up in the middle of the coffee table. All four of the candles were lit, and the four angels flew around at top speed, making the brass bells tinkle. He thought he smelled cookies, too, even though Mary had planned to bake the next day.

Feeling confused by all these things, Andrew came to the door of the den and looked in toward the tree. It was so bright that he found it hard to look at it. The angel on top seemed to be leaning over toward him, and the two tiny candles that she held in her hands burned more brightly than any of the other lights. Everything was just a little strange, but somehow clearer. "Could I be dreaming again? "Andrew wondered.

But before he could answer his own question, something moved near the tree! He was shocked to see that it was a boy about his own age, dressed in white pajamas and blue slippers. The boy was kneeling at the foot of the tree, replacing an ornament that Diggory had knocked off earlier that evening. The boy then turned and smiled, looking as if he had been waiting for Andrew to arrive.

"Hi!" the boy said, as if that was all that he needed to say. The boy looked a little like the picture of Mario that his dad had stuck on the door of the refrigerator. His hair was dark and his eyes bright and sparkling.

Andrew wasn't sure whether to be friendly or to act tough. The situation seemed to call for toughness. So Andrew frowned and asked, "Who are you? And what are you doing here?"

As he looked at the boy, waiting for an answer, he felt a warm glow spreading from the top of his head to the tips of his toes. He seemed to recognize the boy from somewhere, but he could not remember where he'd met him.

"I'm a friend, and I've come to visit," the boy replied, as if it was the most normal thing in the world for someone to come visit you in the middle of the night.

What was odd was that Andrew wanted to accept the boy's explanation without pressing him for more information. He somehow knew that the boy was his friend, that he could trust him, and that to ask any more questions might spoil something that was special and hard to put into words.

"Do you want to play?" the boy asked. It was late and Andrew knew he was supposed to be in bed. But a magical feeling filled the air. Laughing at the idea of playing in the middle of the night, Andrew said, "Sure, but we'd better not wake Dad and Mary up!"

"I don't think they will wake up, but I don't think they would mind either," the boy replied.

"Do you know them?" Andrew asked.

The boy nodded.

For the next hour or so, Andrew and the boy played with the toys that Andrew had piled beside the fireplace to make room for the Christmas tree. As the minutes flew by, Andrew felt happier and happier, as if the boy was the best friend anyone could ever have. Andrew talked about everything—toys, school, parents, and animals. The boy mostly listened, but whenever he talked, he had something interesting to say. Spending time with this friend was kind of like eating as much of your favorite candy as you wanted to eat without getting sick—or playing your favorite game as long as you wanted to without getting tired of it. Pretty soon, Andrew forgot that he really knew nothing about this boy who had appeared mysteriously in his dad's house in the middle of night.

"I have to leave soon," the boy finally said.

Andrew suddenly felt a deep sadness that reminded him of when his father left his mom three years before, and when his grandfather Poppy had died. Andrew became alarmed, afraid that he might never see his new friend again.

"Why don't you stay here 'til morning?" Andrew asked. "My dad could take you home then."

The boy replied, "I really have to leave now, but I may be able to come back. But I will need your help...and it won't be easy."

"What won't be easy?" Andrew became agitated. What was the boy talking about, anyway?

"What I mean is, it won't be easy to do what you have to do if you want me to come back," said the boy.

"What do you mean, what I have to do?" Andrew said with frustration in his voice. Then his curiosity got the best of him, and he asked, "So, what *do* I have to do?" Andrew leaned forward to get a better look at the boy. What he saw surprised him. The boy's eyes looked like a grown-up's eyes.

"I will come back," the boy replied, "*when you have given the perfect gift.*"

As Andrew puzzled over these words, the boy began to blend in with the tree lights. Knowing Andrew was upset by his leaving, the boy said, "Never give up, Andrew—and don't be afraid to ask questions."

The lights became so bright that Andrew could no longer make out the boy's face. He looked away for a moment, and then looked back again, only to see a large blue Christmas ball hanging on the tree where the boy had been standing. As Andrew looked closely at the ball, he saw an opening on the side of the ornament. Through this opening, Andrew could see trees and snow and a dark blue sky, and a big bright star in the distance.

As Andrew tried to find the boy in this tiny nighttime scene, the image of the blue ornament gradually faded away, and he found himself lying in his bed. He realized that he must have been dreaming, but the experience was so vivid and so real that Andrew knew somehow that it had been more than a dream.

Chapter Two
The Mysterious Ornament

The next morning, Andrew woke early and was eager to play with some of his friends. Having forgotten about meeting the stranger, he dressed quickly and bounded down the stairs. He raced through the den, and glanced to see if any new presents were under the Christmas tree.

Then he saw something that startled him. There, in the middle of the tree, was the same blue ornament that he had seen in his dream during the night! When he investigated it closely, he saw that it looked older and much finer than the Christmas balls they'd bought at the store. Instead of hanging from a hook, the ball was tied to the tree with a piece of heavy wire.

Knowing that it hadn't been there the previous day, Andrew went to find Mary, who was working at her computer.

"Mary, do you know where that big blue Christmas ball came from?" Andrew asked.

Mary turned around in her swivel chair, and smiled. "I thought you'd notice it before long," Mary replied. "I hung it on the tree last night after you went to bed. It's been in my family for a long time."

Andrew nodded. "Where did it come from?"

Mary looked into Andrew's eyes for a few moments, and considered whether to tell him the story of the blue ornament. It seemed like only yesterday when her mother first showed her the old faded letter that her father had written to her at the end of World War II. Mary had been only seven years old at the time, and her older brother had left for the Vietnam War the week before. She had been crying off and on for days, not knowing whether she'd ever see her brother again. Her mother had sensed that it was the right time to tell Mary the amazing story of the blue ornament.

Sure enough, her father's wartime letter had given Mary hope that her brother would someday return home safely. However, Mary had never shown the letter to Andrew's father, or even to her own children. She knew that there would come a time to share the letter with each of them, but that it had to be the right time.

Mary sensed that Andrew, being an especially sensitive child, still struggled with sadness over his parents' divorce. Being a light sleeper, she would sometimes hear him talking in his sleep. She realized that the story of the blue ornament might help him.

"I have something to share with you," she said. Mary went to her closet and took out an old dented metal box from the top shelf. Then she led Andrew downstairs to the sofa by the tree. As she opened the dented box, Andrew could see that it was lined with red velvet. Mary reached in and took out a yellowed envelope containing the handwritten letter that her father had sent to her mother over 55 years earlier, after he'd been wounded in the invasion at Normandy.

"Andrew, my father wrote this letter to my mother from France during World War II, just after D-Day. Do you know what that was?"

Andrew nodded. "We just studied that in school. It's when we surprised the Germans with a huge attack."

"My father was wounded early in the in the battle. While he was recovering from his injuries, he met someone who was very special. Do you want to hear his story?"

"Sure." Andrew then snuggled up against Mary as she opened the envelope and took out her father's letter. As she began reading, Andrew closed his eyes and listened.

Dearest Glenna,

Of course, you must know by now that we landed on the beaches of France over a week ago. As we approached the shoreline in the landing crafts, we were all terrified. Our fears were soon justified, for many of my comrades fell wounded in the surf or on the beaches. Many of them died there. Those of us who somehow made it through the machine gun fire could not stop to help them: Our only hope for survival was to find a way to take out the German bunkers. Even so, the cries of my wounded and dying comrades still haunt me.

Much of what happened is a blur now, because I did not get very far before I, too, fell wounded and unconscious. (But please do not worry for me, Glenna. I will soon be as good as new.)

My platoon was taking out a German bunker when a shell exploded nearby. I was knocked unconscious from the explosion and took a bit of shrapnel in my leg. When I awakened almost three days later, I could remember very little about what had happened. I was in a tent hospital outside a little village, and the battle had moved far to the west of us.

Through the opening in my tent flap, I noticed a steeple rising above the village, so when the doctor said it was okay to move about, I set out on foot to find the church. I wanted to practice my French among the local people, and to pray for my fallen friends.

When I arrived at the little church, I discovered that it was attached to a monastery that had been virtually flattened during a tank battle. As I entered the chapel, I was saddened by what I saw. The once-beautiful sanctuary was almost totally destroyed. The stained glass windows had been shattered, and the roof had collapsed in several places.

Before I could turn to leave, however, I noticed that someone had moved a few of the pews closer to the altar. So, on second thought, I decided to stay and say my prayers.

I knelt and began to pray for my comrades, and to give thanks for your love and for God's grace in my life. After a while, I heard someone come into the chapel. When I opened my eyes, I saw a priest in a dusty robe, kneeling before the altar and holding a chalice and a large piece of bread.

You can imagine how I felt when he rose, turned around, and came to give me communion. I said as best I could in French, "Father, I am not a Catholic."

He looked around at the devastation, and then he leaned over and said with a twinkle in his eyes, "God knows what you are." Then he handed me the cup and the bread, and began praying over me. I took the bread and followed it with a healthy portion of the wine. He seemed to approve, for when I had finished, he did the same.

"Andrew," Mary asked, "are you still with me?" Andrew had been sitting so still that Mary thought he might have dozed off.

Andrew opened his eyes with a start, looking very alert. "Yes! Please don't stop now," he said. "I want to hear the whole story." Mary paused for a moment, looking thoughtful. "Let's have a muffin while we read the rest of the story, okay?"

He agreed, suddenly aware that he was very hungry. A little while later after a quick trip to the kitchen, Mary continued reading her father's letter while Andrew gazed at the mysterious blue ornament on the Christmas tree.

For a while, we sat together praying in silence. Then, he went around behind the altar and dislodged a stone from the floor. He returned carrying a dented metal box.

He opened the case, and in the center of the red velvet lining, there was a beautiful object made of glass. The priest took it out and handed it to me. It was, of all things, a beautiful blue ornament—the kind of thing that we might use to decorate a Christmas tree back home.

In the midst of all the suffering and devastation I'd seen, the ornament shone with a delicate beauty that seemed simply miraculous. In fact, it was so beautiful that I held it carefully with both hands, and just stared at it, unable to say anything.

After I looked at it for a minute or two, I gave it back to the priest. He put it back into the box and then handed it to me. He said, "I want you to have this."

I was sure he'd made a mistake. So, I said, "But you don't even know me! Why give it to me?!"

"Why do we do the things that we are called to do?" He shrugged.

"God told you to give it to me?" I asked with utter disbelief.

The priest closed his eyes and said, "I felt it here," touching his heart. "And, what's more, before I leave, I will tell you how this blue ornament came to be made."

Andrew took a sip of his hot chocolate and then turned to Mary. "We're lucky to have the blue ball, aren't we?" Then, he suddenly became worried that it might fall from the tree. "Is that wire strong enough?"

"Don't worry, Andrew," Mary replied, tousling his hair. "It would support even your weight." Then Mary began reading the priest's story from her father's letter.

"After the first World War," the priest said, "a young local man joined our religious order. His father was a master glass blower who had begun to teach his son all of the secrets of his ancient art. In time, everyone expected the young man—who showed great promise—to surpass even his father's skill.

"But then, when he was 19, the young man felt called to give his life to God by becoming a monk. His father was saddened to lose his most gifted apprentice, but he was a devout man, and he gave his son his blessings. Soon, the young man entered the monastery.

"Everything went well, and he was invited to become a full member of our order. In preparation for the ceremony, the young man went out into the fields around the village and picked wildflowers for the altar.

"While walking back to the monastery, he suddenly beheld a vision of a beautiful woman who shone with a blue radiance. Overwhelmed by joy, he knelt before her and laid the flowers at her feet. The lady said nothing, but looked upon him with the expression of a mother's love for her child.

"The young man finally asked, 'How can I serve you?' Smiling, the lady replied, 'By giving the world your most precious gift.'

"Not knowing for sure what that would mean, he simply said, 'I will.' Then, as he gazed upon her, he noticed a blue globe floating beneath her feet that looked like the earth. It resembled many of the glass ornaments he had made before he entered the monastery. He bowed his head and gratitude filled his heart. It was the most beautiful moment of his life. And then, when he looked up again, she was gone.

"When the young man returned from his walk, he went and told our director what he had experienced. Our leader, in his wisdom, interpreted the glorious vision rather literally. He commanded the man to resume his art of glass blowing, so that the world might enjoy his finest gift.

"The young monk was overjoyed. And when his father learned of the wonderful news, he gave his son everything he needed to set up his workshop in our monastery.

Soon, the monk was teaching his fellow monks how to blow glass, and in time our monastery began to depend on the sale of glass ornaments to support our mission to feed the poor."

Then, the priest turned to me with a sober look. "The concussion from the exploding bombs destroyed all of the ornaments that remained here—except for this one that we kept beneath the floor behind the altar. It was the most precious of all the ornaments, for it was the first one that the young monk made after the Lady appeared to him."

As the priest finished his story, Glenna, he rose to leave, and we embraced like brothers. We both wept, and it seemed that our joy and our sorrow mingled together in that sad, sacred place.

When I asked him what he wanted me to do with the ornament, he said, "Let it be a reminder to you of what will always endure."

"But won't you need it?" I asked, as he headed toward the doorway.

"I will make others," he replied without turning. "But none quite as precious as the one that is yours."

As he disappeared, I knew suddenly that I had been talking to the man who had made the blue ornament.

And now, dearest Glenna, I long to see you and to share with you this precious gift.

Love, Michael

Mary folded the letter and put it back in the dented metal box. Both she and Andrew were quiet, for they were both lost in their own thoughts. But after a while, Mary asked,

"Andrew, what do you think about my father's story?"

Andrew went to look at the blue ornament. He tried to put it all together—his experience with the stranger in the night, and now this story about a mysterious glass ornament made by a French monk many years before. It was all very confusing.

Andrew finally said, "I..I don't know, Mary."

Chapter Three
What Fathers Long For

When Andrew came home from playing with his friends, he saw that his door was slightly ajar. "Diggory's been here again!" Sure enough, the fence around his dinosaur compound was down, and the dinosaurs were laying on their sides. Andrew jumped up, ran out the door, and down the hallway. He knew where Diggory liked to hide—beneath the wing chair in the TV room.

"Diggory!" Andrew yelled, and then he saw the culprit's bushy tail sticking out from under wing chair. Andrew reached down to give Diggory's tail a swift tug, but then he thought better of it. His dad would not approve, and it was too near Christmas to risk making him mad.

Christmas was fast approaching, and Andrew had not yet bought any of his presents. But after meeting the stranger in the night, he knew that he wasn't quite ready to go Christmas shopping. After all, he couldn't give a perfect gift unless he first knew what one was. Andrew laid down on the carpet and stared at the ceiling. He didn't know where to start.

When he considered the story about the monk and the blue ornament, Andrew felt envious. When the lady in the vision told the monk to give HIS most precious gift, anyone could figure out what THAT was. The monk was even given a BIG HINT when he saw the blue globe floating at the lady's feet, in case he couldn't figure it out himself. He had a talent that everybody knew about, and all he had to do was get back to work.

But Andrew realized that he was only a kid, and that he wasn't expected to have something beautiful to give away. He concluded that the perfect gift isn't always something great that you already have, but maybe it's perfect because it's exactly what someone needs. So, even though he wished he could make something beautiful that everyone would like, he had to approach the problem differently. He had to give gifts that people wanted or needed.

At first, he considered that there might be only one perfect gift—the same thing for everyone, that is. But the more he thought about it, the more he couldn't imagine buying one thing that would make everybody on his list happy, no matter what the gift was. A tube of lipstick might please Gram and Mom, but certainly not Mary's son, Tommy.

"I can just see Tommy's face if I gave him some red lipstick." Andrew rolled around the floor laughing. "Seeing Tommy open that present would be a perfect gift for me."

But then he stopped laughing. Andrew was worried. How could he discover what the perfect gift would be for everyone on his list? Suddenly, he remembered the boy's words, "Don't be afraid to ask questions." It seemed like an important clue. So Andrew decided to ask each person on his list the question, "What do you think is the perfect gift?" By the answering thc question, maybe they'd make it easy by telling him what to get them.

He went to his desk and after writing down this question in big bold letters, he made a list of the seven people that he wanted to buy presents for: Mom, Cyrus, Dad, Mary, Gram, Tommy, and Sarah. After some hesitation, Andrew included Diggory way down at the end of the list, even though he was still mad at the cat for messing up his toys and for knocking the Christmas balls off the tree.

Diggory had come to them just a few months before, so this was his first Christmas. When Dad, Mary, Tommy, Sarah, and Andrew were up in the Blue Ridge mountains in July, they talked about getting a kitty. Just after leaving for the trip home, they came upon Diggory and four other kittens eating a dead chipmunk in the middle of the road. They thought that this was their chance. Since the kittens were obviously on their own, and not likely to survive for long, they tried to catch one of them. The first one bit Stephen, and the next one outran him. Diggory was the only kitty he could catch, so they took him home with them.

They didn't know it at the time, but they had managed to catch up with him only because he was weak from an incurable disease. He seemed healthy now, but Andrew knew that he wasn't supposed to live as long as a normal cat. Given the people and pets who had left him or died in the last few years, it was hard for Andrew to get very interested in a pet that might not be around for long, especially one that was so misbehaved.

Now, only four days remained before Christmas. Andrew had to move fast if he was going to ask everyone his question in time to buy presents for them. He decided to interview his dad first.

Stephen was sitting on the sofa near the Christmas tree, reading a book about fishing. Andrew sat down beside him and waited for Stephen to look up. Several moments passed, and Andrew considered leaving, but he caught sight of the blue ornament out of the corner of his eye. Once again the boy's voice whispered. "Don't be afraid to ask questions."

"Uh...Dad?"

"What's up, Bud?" Stephen answered dreamily without looking up. He was lost in a story about catching a big rainbow trout.

"I need to ask you a question, Dad." Andrew waited for some sure sign that his dad had heard him.

"Um...okay," Stephen said. Then he closed the book, putting it on the coffee table.

"What's on your mind, Andrew?"

"Dad, here it is: What do you think is the perfect gift?" Andrew asked without looking directly at him. He knew that Stephen would wonder what was going on.

Sure enough, he looked very surprised. He leaned toward his son and asked, "You're asking me about the 'perfect gift,' Andrew?"

"Yes, sir." Andrew waited, hoping that he wouldn't ask any more questions. Not yet, anyway.

Stephen looked at his son in silence, trying to remember where he'd heard that question before. Maybe it was part of some dream he'd forgotten. He felt somehow that Andrew was searching for something that he had looked for, too—something so important that it might change Andrew's life. He wanted for Andrew to tell him why he was asking this question, but he felt that it wasn't the right time. Andrew obviously didn't want to talk. So, Stephen decided that the best thing would be simply to answer the question as best he could.

He leaned back again and looked over his son's head toward the fireplace. He considered in the span of a few moments the 46 years of his life—his happy childhood; the shock of his parents' divorce when he was 16; the joy of adopting Andrew, his only child; his 17-year marriage and his own divorce; and then the joy of meeting and marrying Mary. But Stephen had a problem with feeling sad a lot, and the sadness would sometimes drag him down like an anchor tied to his heart. Stephen realized that if anything was true about his life, it was this: He was never sure if what he did was right. He often doubted himself and became sad and even depressed at times.

"Well, Bud, I guess the perfect gift is love," said Stephen. "What do you think?"

Andrew thought about, then rolled his eyes, realizing that he should have known that this would happen. "Dad, you can't wrap it up. People want something at Christmas, not just love. I mean, love is great, but..." Andrew looked desperate. "I've got only two or three dollars to spend for each person on my list!"

"I see your problem." After thinking about it a little longer, Stephen said, "Maybe you need to change the question. Because any adult would probably say the same thing. And then, on top of that, when you ask Tommy and Sarah, they might say that the perfect gift would be something huge and expensive. An answer like that won't help you either, will it?"

Andrew looked even more worried. His dad made it sound impossible. "What can I do? Do you have any ideas?" he asked.

Stephen thought for a moment. "Well, it seems to me that a perfect gift is something that *does* something to you, that makes you feel a certain way. The gift itself could be lots of things, really."

Andrew picked up on the idea and said, "So...a perfect gift would do something for you, or make you feel good?" He was getting excited now, because they seemed to be on the verge of solving the puzzle.

His dad looked into the fire for a while and then turned to Andrew. "I think you just said it. Try putting it into a question and see if that feels right."

Andrew thought a minute, and said slowly, "What would the perfect gift *do* for you?"

Stephen nodded. "That's it!"

"Great!" Andrew shouted. "Okay, so will you please answer the question, Dad?"

Stephen leaned forward again. As he considered the new question, he suddenly thought of one of his counseling patients.

"Andrew, I once had a patient named Lydia. Her mother left her and her little brother in an orphanage when they were very young. So Lydia grew up thinking that she was unwanted and unlovable. She was so depressed that she even tried to kill herself one time. Well, we worked really hard to keep her from doing that again.

And, one day her husband had to go away on a business trip. He'd never left Lydia by herself, because he was afraid that she'd hurt herself while he was away. Since she was doing better, we all decided that he should go on his trip and that Lydia and I would stay in touch over the weekend."

"Wow, that was taking a big risk, huh, Dad?" Andrew asked.

"It sure was." Stephen put his arm around his son. "But anyway, I called her every few hours to make sure she was okay. And she called me a couple of times, too. But at the end of the second day, I called and there was no answer. I became worried. So I got in my car and found where they lived. I knocked on the door and shouted her name. But no one came. I was afraid she was already dead. Desperately, I kept pounding on the door, shouting her name. Finally, just before I was going to call 911, the door opened, and there was Lydia looking very embarrassed. You see, she was hard of hearing, and she had removed her hearing aids. Well, she invited me in and gave me some tea, grateful and pleased that I had cared enough to come to check on her."

Stephen paused, smiling to himself. "Oddly enough, from that day onward she improved very rapidly. She told me later that my coming out that day helped her to realize that she really mattered to people.

"What's amazing was how I didn't plan it," Stephen continued.. "It was just one of those 'accidents' that made someone feel better. She became well enough in time that she quit coming for counseling. And now she's pretty much okay."

Stephen became silent for a moment, and Andrew tried not to fidget because he knew his father was thinking.

"Anyway, Andrew, I think the perfect gift for me would make *me* always feel what Lydia felt that day—that I am a good person and deserve love. Like Lydia felt that day. How's that?"

Andrew was not surprised that his dad would say something like that. He had once overheard his mother talking about it to a friend on the phone, back when things were really unpleasant. She had said, "He will never be happy." These words had struck fear in Andrew's heart, and he hoped that his mom had been wrong about his dad. However, Andrew knew that his dad would sometimes go into his bedroom by himself. He would come out looking tired and older, sometimes with red eyes. He never talked to Andrew about it, but there were times Andrew wanted to follow his dad into the room and try to make him feel better if he could.

His father's answer gave Andrew some hope that he'd be able to find a perfect little gift that would do just that for his dad.

Andrew started writing and asked Stephen to repeat the answer a couple more times before he had written down all of the words in the space he'd left between

"Dad" and "Mary" on his list. He looked very serious when he looked up and said, "Thank you, Dad."

Before Andrew left, his father asked, "Will you tell me how you came up with this idea? It's really interesting."

Andrew smiled. "Sure, but I'd rather wait until Christmas, okay? It's kind of a secret."

"Sure, Bud," Stephen nodded, feeling proud of his son.

The next morning, Andrew went to church with his mom and Cyrus. He liked some of the songs and some of what the preacher had to say, but he disliked the children's part of the service. It always seemed kind of silly to him. So while all the other kids gathered around the minister, Andrew tried to look older and kept his seat beside his Mom and Cyrus.

His thoughts turned to what he might be getting for Christmas. But he couldn't think about all of that for very long before his experience with the strange boy came back. The mystery of the perfect gift constantly bothered him. Maybe he'd find the answer—at least for one of the people on his list. After all, the boy didn't mean that he had to give the perfect gift to everyone—did he?

He turned and looked at his stepfather sitting beside him. Towering above the people around him, Cyrus reminded Andrew of one of the big pine trees in the front yard, and he wondered if Cyrus ever felt weird sticking up so high that everybody could see him. And, what's more, he didn't have much hair.

"I'd slump," Andrew thought.

After the service, they stopped for lunch, and then went home. Andrew turned on the TV, and his mom took out a book to read. Cyrus went up to his office, as usual, for he worked almost every day, even on Sunday. A little while later, Andrew took his pencil and notebook and went to see him. Andrew knew that Cyrus was often busy on the computers, so he wasn't sure it was a good time to ask him the question.

Andrew stood in the door of the little bedroom that was filled with computers and other stuff that he barely understood. Even though it was a small room, Cyrus didn't look so big in there. If he was like a pine tree, then the computers and monitors were like skyscrapers that surrounded him and made him look like the only natural thing left in some future world where all the other trees had been turned into paper and toothpicks.

Cyrus brought Andrew's fantasy to an end by looking up and smiling. No matter how busy he was, he was always kind to Andrew.

"What can I do for you, Andrew?" he asked. He had just turned on one of the computers, and the whirring and clicking sounds told Andrew that it would be a while before Cyrus could use it.

"I've got a very important question that I'm asking some people to answer," Andrew said. "You're one of them, okay?"

"Sure, what is it?" Cyrus waited.

"Cyrus, what would the perfect gift do for you?" Andrew asked. He looked intently at Cyrus, holding his pencil to the paper.

"Wow, that's a big one. Now, let's see." Cyrus looked down for a moment, thinking over the events of the last year. He had married Andrew's mom soon after his best friend and business partner, Carl had died. Cyrus' house in New Hampshire remained unsold, full of his partner's furniture and clothing. On top of that, the business success that he'd hoped for kept slipping out of his grasp. But he worked hard every day and every night, trying to make his business grow. Meanwhile, Cyrus had been unable to take much time off to spend with his new family. He sighed, and looked up at Andrew, who hadn't moved.

"Andrew, when my partner Carl found out that he had cancer, he started writing to old friends and getting in touch with his family. He started giving money to the poor and wanted to spend more time talking with me about life and important things.

"One day he said to me, 'Cyrus, don't do what I have done. Don't wait to spend time with those you love. I'm lucky. I still have a year or so before I'll be gone. But I wish I'd spent more time with the people that I love.'"

When Carl finally died, Cyrus, Jane, and Andrew went out on a boat and spread his ashes over the waters of the Chesapeake Bay. It's what Carl had wanted. After watching Carl die at the age of 51, and hearing his words of advice, Cyrus knew that he was still not doing what Carl had advised him to do. So he ended his story by saying, "Andrew, I would say that the perfect gift would make it easier for me to spend a little more time with the people I love."

Tears glistened in Cyrus' eyes. Andrew suspected that Cyrus missed spending more time with his mom, but he felt a little shy about asking him more.

Andrew wrote the words down and began to worry. Cyrus' answer seemed even tougher than his dad's had been. How could he ever find the perfect gift for people who gave him such complicated answers? He felt discouraged, but the stranger's words, "Never, never give up," echoed in his mind. So, he put his notebook under his arm, and went to find his mom.

Chapter Four
What Mothers Seek

As he went looking for his mom, Andrew remembered a dream that he had the night before. In the dream, he saw his grandfather, who had passed away the previous year. Poppy was standing beside Tippy across a stream. Tippy was his mom's Collie that had died in September. In the dream, both Poppy and Tippy were alive and happy again. Poppy smiled and waved, and Tippy ran around, looking and acting like a puppy. Then, off to the side, Andrew saw Diggory getting ready to jump across the narrow stream to join them.

Andrew missed Poppy. He was a wonderful grandfather. He had spent long hours with Andrew—wrestling with him, taking him fishing, building things for him, cooking beans in tin cans over campfires, and reading to him until one of them would fall asleep. But now, Poppy was gone.

For a while after Poppy died, Andrew would imagine talking to him when he was alone. But recently, Andrew had begun to forget the sound of Poppy's voice. When that happened, he looked at Poppy's picture over the fireplace to remind himself of what Poppy looked like and that made him feel better. The dreams also helped him feel close to Poppy, because they were so real. But Andrew sometimes saw things in his dreams that came true later. So, dreaming of Poppy reassured him, but seeing Diggory trying to join Poppy and Tippy on the other side of the stream made Andrew worry that he might be leaving them, too.

Carrying his notebook and pencil, Andrew went out into the side yard. His mother sat under the grape trellis on the wooden bench, reading an old English novel.

It was one of those delicious days when early winter steps aside and gives the sun one last chance to warm the earth. The smell of English boxwoods and pine needles mingled in the still, warm air. Andrew's mother enjoyed the earthy smells and the comforting warmth of the delightful day. But her pale skin could not bear the sun's rays, so she sat in the shade of the leafless grape vines, wearing a straw bonnet.

Andrew walked up and plopped to the ground in front of the bench.

"Come on up here, sweetie," his mom said, patting the seat beside her. So Andrew got up and sat down on the bench.

After hugging his mom, he picked up his notebook and said, "Mom, can I ask you a very important question?"

Surprised by her son's seriousness, she said, "Of course, Andrew."

"Mom, here's the question: What would the perfect gift do for you?" Andrew closed the notebook so she wouldn't see all the names on his list.

Jane was amazed and wondered who might be behind Andrew asking such an adult-sounding question. Maybe his Sunday school teacher, she thought. Regardless, she set her book aside and put her arm around her only child.

She knew that she did not handle changes very well. In fact, she disliked any kind of surprise. If someone said, "Boo," she jumped every time just as high as the last time, and it was never, ever funny to her.

Old familiar things comforted Jane. She put her shoes in their original boxes every night and made them last for years. She still wore clothes she bought 25 years before when she was in high school, and she never spent much money on herself. She drove a car until it was old and totally worn out. She cherished whatever was hers, without ever thinking about replacing it.

Above all, she missed the comfort that she felt when her father was alive, and when the whole family would spend time together over the holidays. It was different now. The family didn't visit as much any more.

As she pondered Andrew's question, she spoke to him of her family's past.

"Andrew, do you remember when Poppy was still alive, that we would drive to New York every Christmas to be with the family?"

"Of course I do," Andrew replied. But he was much younger then, and the memory was already fading.

"As you may remember, when we arrived, the tree would already be up, touching the ceiling and sparkling with lights." Jane looked up through the tree branches, relishing the memories. "And," she continued, "an old electric train would be circling the base of the tree. One of those Christmas balls that make chirping noises like a bird would serenade us while we'd sit in the kitchen eating Gram's Christmas cookies and sandwiches from the local delicatessen. And then we'd go out for Italian food on Christmas Eve, remember?"

Andrew nodded slowly. His memory was coming back. He was back in New York, once again experiencing those good times.

She went on. "And then, before we went to bed on Christmas Eve, Poppy would read from *A Christmas Carol*, or we'd watch the movie *It's a Wonderful Life* on the TV. Your Uncle John would almost always fall asleep lying on the floor. We did the same wonderful things every year. You could rely on Poppy and Gram to make the holidays exactly as they had always been. But now that Poppy's gone..." Her voice trailed off, and she bit her lip to keep it from trembling.

"Andrew, I suppose that the perfect gift would make those experiences possible again." Her eyes glistened, and Andrew knew that she was thinking about Poppy.

After carefully writing her words down in his book, Andrew said, "I'll tell you what this is about later, Mom. For now, it's kind of a secret."

"I'd like to hear about it, sweetie, but only when you want to tell me," Jane said.

Andrew left his mom sitting under the grape vines and followed the path to the house. He had no idea what he could do to fulfill his mother's dream, but there wasn't time to worry about it now. The next person on his list was his grandmother.

Gram was sitting in front of the TV, watching her favorite game show. Andrew liked it, too, so he watched the show with her until it was over. Then he said, "Gram, I've got a question to ask. Would you answer it?"

"Of course, Andrew. What's this about?" Dolores sat in her usual place on the love seat by the lamp. A crossword puzzle book lay face down on the cushion beside her, and cookie crumbs were sprinkled around her feet on the Oriental rug. The arthritis in her ankles made it difficult for her to move around anymore, and there was a wrinkle over her brow from the pain that she lived with all the time. She always tried to give Andrew her undivided attention, but sometimes the pain got in the way.

"Gram, here's the question: What would the perfect gift do for you?"

Dolores was a little surprised by such a question, and she felt some reluctance to answering it. She rarely considered what she really wanted for herself. She had learned to keep her own wishes hidden early in her life.

Dolores finally replied by saying, "Andrew, I've never told you about when I was a little girl, but my father didn't seem to like me very much, even though he treated my sister like a princess." She stopped, not sure whether she should continue.

Andrew said, "That must have really hurt your feelings, Gram."

Sensing that he could handle the rest of the story, Dolores continued. "One day, my father returned from a business trip and gave my sister a beautiful little doll, but he brought nothing for me. I was so upset that when no one was looking, I tore the doll apart, knowing full well that it would enrage my dad when he found out. Sure enough, he gave me quite a whipping for what I had done. After that, everything seemed different. I didn't play or laugh as much as before."

She stared out the window and sat quietly for a while before turning back to Andrew. Then she said, "To answer your question, I guess the perfect gift would make me feel as happy as I was before I made my father so angry." Then she wondered how he could possibly make sense of her answer.

Andrew just stared at Gram at first. "Wow," he thought. "This is like Mission Impossible!" But he dutifully began writing down her words, asking her to repeat them until he had them exactly as she had said them.

Later that day, Andrew went back to his dad's house to help Mary bake the Christmas cookies. Mary gave Andrew the "sprinkles" duty. He waited until the soft, warm, chocolate chip cookies came out of the oven, and then he poured sprinkles over each cookie before they hardened. Because Andrew had not been especially careful, more sprinkles decorated the floor than the cookies. But Mary didn't mind.

As she cooked, Andrew noticed that Mary seemed far away at times. He figured that she looking forward to seeing her kids, who would be coming in a couple of days. It had been over four months since she'd seen Tommy and Sarah, and she was often on the phone with them. Andrew thought Mary was really cool. Even though she wasn't Andrew's real mom, she treated him like one of her own kids, and he loved her as much as he could love anyone who had come along later in his life. She didn't argue with his dad, and she was always reasonable with Andrew. Sure, she made him eat things that he didn't want to eat, and she made him do his chores when he forgot to do them. But she did it in a way that almost made it fun. She could be firm, but there was never any doubt that she loved him—and liked him, too.

"Mary, will you answer a very important question?" Andrew asked, while he waited to decorate a fresh batch of cookies. "I will if I can. Go ahead," Mary replied, licking cookie batter off her fingers. She had streaks of flour in her hair, and some sprinkles on her upper lip.

"What would the perfect gift do for you?" Andrew asked. He opened his notebook and waited for her answer.

Mary was pleased that her father's story had made Andrew think about the meaning of the lady's words to the young monk. But it was also clear that Andrew had done some additional thinking to come up with this particular question.

She looked down and far away as if she was looking into a deep well. She was thankful for each day, because it was the first time in years she'd really been happy. And her kids were coming in just three days! She thought back over her marriage with their father—how she'd tried to be a supermom, staying in her marriage even though her husband had treated her meanly. She thought it was important to her children to have both parents around—at least until they were older. When Mary left, Tommy and Sarah were old enough to make their own decisions about where to live. And because they did not want to leave their friends, they stayed behind when their mom moved away to take a job. It was the right decision for them, but she missed them terribly.

As Mary pondered Andrew's question, and how much she longed to be with her children, she remembered Miss Shirley, a neighbor whom Mary spent a lot of time with in her childhood.

"Andrew, when I was a little girl, there was an elderly lady who lived next door. I don't know why, but she took a special interest in me, maybe because I was the daughter she never had. Anyway, I could go and talk with her at any time. She was always so loving and kind." Mary sighed. "I've always felt that she was near me, even though I could be hundreds of miles away from her."

Mary brushed her cheek with the back of her hand, covering it with a light dusting of flour. Then she turned back to the cookie dough, placing a spoonful on thc baking sheet. She paused, holding a spoonful of dough in the air.

"Andrew, I want to be like Miss Shirley more than anything else. So, to answer your question, I believe that the perfect gift would make it possible for the people I love to feel my love no matter how far apart we are."

He wrote down her words in the space below her name and put the notebook down as a new sheet of cookies came out of the oven. Then he applied the sprinkles more carefully, suddenly aware of the mess he had made.

As he thought about the answers the adults had given him, Andrew realized that they had told him the same thing in different ways. They all wanted to be with someone or have something precious that they dearly missed.

And the perfect gift, in every case, would bring them back together again.

Chapter Five
What Children Dream Of

The day before Christmas Eve, Tommy and Sarah arrived from Indiana. Andrew had met them over the summer, so they were already good friends. Sarah became an instant big sister, and she liked Andrew a whole lot. She always knew just what to say to make Andrew open up and talk. She wanted to work with kids when she got out of college, either as a counselor or an art teacher.

Tommy, on the other hand, was a giant six-foot-two-inch, sixteen-year-old kid who treated Andrew pretty well most of the time, but not always. Sometimes they'd fight over little things like what to watch on the TV or who would get the last piece of pizza, and then they'd have to spend some time cooling off. Andrew's dad told him that big brothers were like that, and that Andrew—being an only child—needed to learn how to get along with bigger kids who would not let him get away with just anything. Andrew did not like that idea. But most of the time he secretly enjoyed having a brother and a sister.

That evening the whole family gathered in the den. Christmas carols played on the stereo, and the tree sparkled like magic. But seeing the tree reminded Andrew that he needed to finish his research soon, so he could go shopping. He had to get Sarah and Tommy to cooperate. Knowing Tommy would be the toughest to convince, he went over and sat by Tommy, and finally said, "Hey, Tommy. I've got a question for you." Andrew tried to make it sound like no big deal, because he was afraid Tommy might get suspicious and refuse to answer his question.

Sure enough, Tommy looked at Andrew with squinted eyes. "Is this a joke or something?" he asked.

Tommy liked Andrew, but Andrew was always making fun of him. On the way home from the airport, Andrew had imitated a British accent, and he went on and on needling Tommy with a voice that sounded like a college professor. Andrew had even called Tommy a "mutant." Tommy just laughed, too, not knowing what to say. He knew Andrew was smart and enjoyed his cleverness—most of the time. But sometimes he went too far, and Tommy didn't always know what to do to shut him up without getting into trouble.

"No, it's not a joke." Andrew replied.

"Then fire," Tommy said, since Andrew seemed sincere .

"So if you received the perfect gift, what would it do for you?" Andrew tried not to smile.

"What kind of question is that?! What's a 'perfect gift,' anyway?" Tommy waited a bit for Andrew to admit it was all a joke, but Andrew just sat with his pen in his hand, ready to write whatever Tommy said. "You want to know what would this so-called 'perfect gift' would do for me, huh?" Tommy repeated.

Andrew nodded seriously. "It's an important puzzle," he added.

Tommy decided that Andrew wasn't playing a trick on him. So he closed his eyes for a minute, thinking about the strange question. He felt pretty relaxed here in Virginia with his mom and Stephen, but he didn't feel that way very often back home. He and his dad argued all the time, and Tommy felt he couldn't do anything right, even when he tried hard to please his dad.

Tommy dreamed of being free, of owning his own car so that he could drive wherever he wanted to go. He was even thinking about giving up baseball just so he could work and save up enough money to buy and fix up his own car. But really, deep down, he just wanted peace. He knew that his mom could never get along with his dad, especially toward the end of the marriage. But Tommy hoped that one day he could do what his mom had been unable to do.

Tommy finally said, “Okay, I’ll answer the question. But you have to promise not to make fun of me. Deal?”

“Deal,” said Andrew.

Tommy leaned forward and rested his elbows on his knees. Then he said, “Andrew, you’ve got it good here, because you and your dad get along. You don’t realize how hard it is for me not to fight with my dad. If something goes wrong back home—like if I make a failing grade in school—my dad is instantly in my face yelling at me. It’s hard to tell him the truth all the time because I’m afraid that he’s going to overreact. But then, when he finds out that I’ve not told him things, he gets even madder. We can’t seem to stop fighting.”

Tommy stared straight ahead and then in a low voice said, “I guess the perfect gift would help me not fight with my dad.” Tommy suddenly felt a little choked up, so he quickly changed the subject. “Hey, the cat’s playing with your Legos again.”

But Andrew ignored Diggory for once and began writing in his notebook. “Thanks, Tommy!” Andrew said.

“No problem,” Tommy replied. But he looked away, feeling embarrassed. Andrew’s question had stirred a deep sadness within him, and Tommy did not know what to do with these feelings. Instead he withdrew from the conversation and sat quietly looking at the fire.

One more person, Andrew thought. Then I have only one day to do everything. He tried not to panic.

Sarah proved to be a lot more willing than Tommy to talk. All he had to say was, "Sarah, will you answer a very important question for me?" She put her arm around him, and said, "Sure." Just like that. It was amazing, Andrew thought, just how much easier it was to get girls to talk.

"Sarah, what would the perfect gift do for you?" Andrew grabbed his pencil and waited for her answer.

Sarah realized that she was the last one to answer this strange question. Everyone seemed to be waiting to hear what she had to say.

She looked down at the white band of skin on her ring finger, where Elliot's high school ring had been for the last two years. She once thought that the perfect gift would be his wedding ring. But now she knew that a wedding ring could never be the perfect gift, because that depended on someone else loving her and never changing his mind. No, a ring from someone else would be nice, but it would never again seem like the perfect gift. Even so, she did wish for something permanent, something that could never be taken away. Maybe that's impossible, she thought. But she knew she'd never stop longing for it.

Some relationships needed to end, she realized. In fact, she was relieved when her mom and dad split up two years before. But it still hurt to see the family break apart.

Then Sarah spoke to Andrew. "You know what it's like to see your family break up, don't you?"

Andrew nodded with a sad expression.

"Well, when my mom left, I knew it was the best thing. But it still really hurt. And even now, two years later, I sometimes wish that everything could be the way it once was. I still get upset because it was all taken from me."

"It never goes away, does it?" Andrew asked.

"Not entirely, even though it gets better over time. So...I guess I would say that the perfect gift would be something that I'd never have to give up—something that I could keep no matter what. So...what would it do for me?" Sarah paused. "I guess it would make me feel that I would never be completely alone, and that I could rely on myself to make myself happy." Then she smiled at Andrew, as if she had discovered something that she didn't know before.

Andrew closed his notebook, satisfied that he'd gotten all the answers that he needed. So he got up and said good night. Everyone answered, except Tommy who was still sitting quietly looking away from the others, with a troubled look on his face.

"Night, Tommy!" Andrew repeated, thinking that Tommy had simply not heard him. But then Tommy got up abruptly, walked quickly through the kitchen without saying anything, and went out the back door.

Andrew realized that something was wrong. "Did I do something wrong?" he wondered. He stood in the doorway to the den, not knowing what to do. Mary hurried past him.

"Did I do something wrong? Why is he mad?"

"He's not mad, Andrew. He's confused," Sarah explained. "He's been through a lot and he's scared."

"How do you know that?" Andrew asked. "He didn't say anything!"

"Because I'm his sister, and sometimes I feel that same way," Sarah answered.

Chapter Six
What Only Brothers Can Give

Andrew could hear Mary and Tommy talking loudly outside the back door, but he couldn't make out all the words, so he tiptoed through the kitchen and listened from behind the half-open door. Sarah went past him and stood beside her mom on the back steps.

"Tommy, what's wrong? Where are you going?" Mary's voice trembled. She stood barefoot on the steps in her robe, and knew that she could not keep up with Tommy on foot if he decided to leave the yard.

"I don't know, but I need to get away for a while," Tommy said. "I don't belong here. I don't belong anywhere!"

"What do you mean? I want you here with us, Tommy!" Mary felt a sick pain in her chest.

"Mom, this where you belong. But you left us. And now Dad and I fight all the time, just like you did. And he's getting ready to move up north, and he wants me to go with him. I'm going to have to leave all my friends. It's just not fair!" Tommy threw up his hands, in a gesture of helplessness. "Can't you see, Mom? I don't belong anywhere. You have a new family, but I don't!" Then, Tommy turned and started to walk away.

Sarah called after Tommy, afraid that her little brother might go off and do something foolish. "Tommy, I know how you feel, but this is our new family. Give it a chance, okay?" Sarah was aware that she was talking to herself, too, because sometimes she didn't feel like she belonged anywhere either.

Usually Tommy listened to his older sister, but not this time. As he disappeared into the darkness, Mary stepped outside and followed Tommy down the driveway. A cold wind blew, whipping her robe about her legs, but Mary didn't notice. She'd lost her son once before when he refused to go with her, and now it looked like she was losing him again. She called after him. "I have always wanted you with me, Tommy! Don't you remember?" She asked. "I begged you to come with me when I left, but you chose to stay. I never stopped wanting you to be with me." She paused at the mailbox, leaning against it for support. "Please, come back!" she pleaded.

But Tommy kept going, without looking back at his mother. Mary turned and slowly returned to the house. She stepped into the garage, crying uncontrollably. Sarah wrapped her arms around her mother and cried, too.

Andrew felt a great sadness welling up inside him. This is not the way it is supposed to be, he thought sadly. We're supposed to be happy at Christmas.

He stepped aside as Mary and Sarah entered the kitchen. Mary kissed him on the cheek. "Don't worry, Andrew," she said, "you didn't do anything wrong. It will be okay. Tommy will come back." She glanced at the doorway.

Stephen put his arms around her and hugged her gently. "Let him go, Mary. He needs some time. He'll be back, soon. I am sure of that," Stephen said.

"Me, too, Mom," Sarah chimed in.

Mary nodded wearily and then looked at the clock on the stove. "You two need to go to bed soon. Don't forget to brush your teeth, Andrew."

Andrew knew better than to fuss. He hugged Mary and said good night.

"I'll tuck him in, Mary," Stephen said. "You try to get some sleep, too. I'll be there shortly."

Sarah said good night, but instead of going to bed she went out onto the front porch for a while. As Andrew passed the front door on his way to his room, he saw Sarah leaning over the edge of the railing. He knew she was hoping to catch sight of Tommy heading back to the house. She looked almost as sad as Mary did. He felt a heaviness in his chest, and he wanted it to go away. He didn't want anyone in his family to ever feel sad again.

He went up into his room and sat on the floor next to his dinosaur herd. At first, it made him feel better to imagine that everything was just the way it had been only an hour before. But he could not shake off the sadness that he felt, nor forget the words that he heard Tommy say—"I don't belong anywhere." Tommy's words haunted Andrew, because they made him remember all over again the one day that he wished he could forget forever—the day that his dad left.

Andrew realized that he often felt the same way that Tommy did. "Sometimes I feel like I don't belong anywhere, either," he said out loud. Then with a sigh, he climbed into bed, but he just wasn't able to sleep.

He laid in the darkness, feeling more and more desperate. He wanted to do something that would turn this Christmas into what it was supposed to be. As he considered what he could do, an idea suddenly came to him. He looked around and found the baby stegosaurus grazing with his parents. He picked it up and ran down the hallway to Tommy's room. He wasn't completely sure what he was going to do, but for some reason, he wanted to give the dinosaur to Tommy.

When he got to the room where Tommy stayed when he was visiting, Andrew stopped at the open door and looked in. Tommy's suitcase lay on the floor, and his clothes were scattered everywhere. An old, worn baseball glove lay on his pillow.

"What a mess!" Andrew said.

Then he noticed that Tommy's bat bag was on the bed as well and that several bats were half way under the covers. "He sleeps with his bats!" Andrew shook his head. "Weird!" Of course, Andrew did not stop to consider the strange assortment of animals and toy guns and candy wrappers that regularly accompanied him to bed. He sat on the bed for a moment before deciding to wait by the door for Tommy to return. Andrew had always wanted to be a Marine like his grandfather Poppy had been, so he pretended that he was keeping guard on Tommy's room.

He stood at attention with his chin down and his body rigid...for maybe one minute. Then he realized that even the best soldiers have to sit down every once in a while. So he sat down cross-legged with his back flat against the wall. He instructed the baby stegosaurus to stand at attention, too. Two minutes later, Andrew decided that the best soldiers can remain at attention even while lying down if they keep their back perfectly straight and their hands at their sides.

Within a minute, Andrew was fast asleep.

At first Tommy walked to the end of the road and looked into the gum thicket near the creek. It was wet and dark—no place to be on a cold night. Tommy shivered and hurried back up the other side of the street, not sure what to do. Ahead of him, near the entrance to the subdivision, he spotted an elderly man walking his dog. The man stopped and looked up at the overhanging trees, as the dog carefully inspected the base of the street lamp.

Tommy slowed his pace as he approached the man and dog. "Good evening, sir," Tommy said.

"Evenin' son. I'm Mr. Fentress, and this is Jack."

"Hi Mr. Fentress. I'm Tommy. Mrs. MacLean is my mom."

"Good to know you, Tommy. Are you visiting for Christmas?" Mr. Fentress asked.

"Yeh, my sister and I will be here until after New Year's." Tommy shivered, aware suddenly that he only had his jeans and sweatshirt on.

"It's a cold night to be out taking a walk," the man said, and he looked closely at Tommy briefly, squinting. "Jack here doesn't think it's too cold, but I'm looking forward to that fireplace already."

"I just wanted to...get out for a while," Tommy said, reaching down to scratch Jack's ears. Jack smelled Tommy's leg with obvious interest.

"Looks like Jack smells that crazy cat of yours." He pointed his cane toward the path. "Walk with me a bit, if you will."

Tommy nodded, tucked his hands into the pockets of his jeans, and walked next to the man. A cold wind whipped a light dusting of snow around them, and Tommy shivered.

"I can remember needing to take a break," Mr. Fentress said. "I used to come out here, too, when my wife was still alive, whenever...we had a difference of opinion." Mr. Fentress shook his head.

Tommy glanced at the old man and then quickly looked away.

"I sure miss her," Mr. Fentress said sadly.

They walked a little while in silence, and then Jack stopped at a fire hydrant in front of the MacLean house.

"I guess you'd better get back home now," Mr. Fentress said. "It's too cold to be out here without your coat, don't you think?"

"Yes sir, time to go in." Tommy replied.

"Merry Christmas, Tommy. Give your mom and...dad...my best wishes," Mr. Fentress said.

"Merry Christmas to you, too, sir," Tommy said, reaching out to give Jack a scratch behind the ears. "And...thanks."

Mr. Fentress said nothing, but gave Tommy a knowing smile before he and Jack continued their walk.

A few minutes later, Tommy entered through the back door and headed quietly up the dark stairs to the guest room. He was tired, and he just wanted to go to sleep.

Suddenly, he saw something on the floor in the darkness, and jumped back. "Geez," he gasped. Then he leaned closer to take a look. It was too big to be Diggory. Inching closer to the strange lump, Tommy then heard a familiar voice call out in the darkness, "At your service, sir!"

Tommy turned on the light over the stairway and saw that it was Andrew lying on his back beside his doorway, blinking and saluting.

"What are you doing here?" Tommy asked.

"Waiting for you to come back, sir. I brought you a present, sir."

Tommy thought that Andrew was overdoing the "sir" bit, but he figured that Andrew felt foolish lying there on the floor and needed to sound like he'd planned it all. Andrew sat up, still holding his right hand rigidly to his brow, and handed Tommy the baby stegosaurus.

"He is the only dinosaur that I have who has a family. I thought you'd like to have him."

"At ease, soldier," Tommy said, hoping that Andrew would not call him "sir" again. He was beginning to see what Andrew was up to. "You heard what I said to my mom, huh?"

Andrew nodded. "I want you to feel like you belong here."

Tommy went into the room and sat on the bed, moving the bats aside to make some room for Andrew. "Thanks, but it's not that easy, Andrew."

Andrew sat on the bed, facing Tommy,. "I know it isn't. I don't feel like I belong here a lot of the time, either."

"But you belong here," Tommy insisted. "Most of your friends live around here. Your mom only lives a few blocks away, and your parents get along, and..."

Andrew interrupted him with a surprised look. "Not all the time!"

"Well, they get along better than mine did," Tommy insisted. "At least your parents talk about important things once in awhile."

"Tommy, I really don't feel that I belong anywhere sometimes. It's not just because of the divorce." He looked around the room. "It's because...you see..." He sighed. Then he blurted out, "I was adopted." There, he'd finally said it! He turned away, afraid of seeing Tommy's reaction.

"Nuh, uh! No way!" Tommy said. "You look like your dad!" Then he saw that Andrew was serious. "Really? When? I mean, how old were you?" Tommy struggled for the right words, feeling awkward about asking such questions.

"Mom and Dad had a friend who knew this girl who wasn't married and got pregnant. She wanted to find a home for me before I was born. So Mom and Dad agreed to adopt me." Andrew walked over to the window and then went on with his story.

"Mom and Dad came to the hospital just after I was born, and they took me home when I was only a couple days old." Andrew explained. "I never knew my real mom." He put his hands over his face and said with a shaky voice, "Dad once told me that my real mom refused to hold me because she was afraid she'd want to take me home with her."

Tommy watched Andrew struggling with his emotions. It made him uncomfortable.

"Sometimes I wish that she would have held me just once." Andrew stared out the window.

Tommy was stunned. He sat silently for a while, and suddenly felt very close to Andrew. We are a lot alike, he realized.

Then Andrew looked squarely at his stepbrother and said, "If I belong here, then you belong, too. Right?"

Tommy had to admit that it made sense. He nodded slowly. "I guess so."

"This is your home as much as it is mine," Andrew said.

Tommy smiled at Andrew's generosity, and then felt a sudden urge to give something to Andrew. At first he had no idea what he could give him. Then it came to him. He went into his bat bag and pulled out his oldest and smallest bat, the one he'd used in Little League. He had always kept it for good luck. He ran his hand across the worn metal and then turned to Andrew. "This is yours now."

Andrew was shocked. He took it from Tommy and held it very carefully. "I'll always take care of it," he promised.

Tommy patted Andrew's back. "You couldn't hurt it if you tried. Just don't hit rocks with it." Then, realizing how late it was, Tommy said, "It's time you got to bed. C'mon, I'll tuck you in."

Together they went down the hall to the other end of the house. Tommy carried the little stegosaurus, and Andrew cradled the old bat in his arms like it was a newborn baby. Andrew went into his room, crawled into his bed, and laid the old bat beside him. Tommy pulled the covers over him. “Good night, Bud. I’ll see you in the morning.”

Tommy turned off the light as he left Andrew’s room. Then he crossed the hallway, taking a deep breath as he stood outside Mary and Stephen’s room. He tapped on the door lightly.

He heard his mom say, “Come in.”

He opened the door and saw Mary sitting in her dark blue chair. She was holding onto a chain of little beads, and her eyes were red and swollen, but now she smiled brightly. Stephen was propped up in bed, but had fallen asleep.

“Mom...” Tommy paused. “I’m home now.”

Mary nodded, knowing that somehow a little miracle had taken place. She rose from the chair and hugged her son.

Stephen suddenly woke up and saw Mary and Tommy hugging at the foot of the bed. He smiled. “Hey, welcome home!”

“It’s good to be here.” Tommy replied. “I’m sorry I upset you guys. I just had to get out for a little while.”

“We understand, Tommy,” Stephen reassured him. “You get some sleep now. I’m sure your mom will have us busy tomorrow with some last-minute holiday preparations."

"Good night," Tommy said, with a smile on his face as he closed the door to their room.

As Tommy turned to go back down the hall, he looked at the dinosaur in his hand and had a sudden thought. He stuck his head into Andrew's room.

"Hey, Andrew. Do you mind if I keep the baby steg here with his mom and dad? I mean, he'd probably feel better staying here with them."

"Yeh, that's a great idea," Andrew answered sleepily. "Just remember he's yours, okay?"

"Okay," Tommy answered, and he put the little dinosaur down on the carpet in between the two larger stegosauruses.

"Night, Andrew."

"Night."

And then, feeling happier than he'd felt in a long, long time, Tommy headed back to his room, stopping momentarily at Sarah's door to see if she was still awake. Hearing nothing, he said ever so gently, "Good night, sis. I love you." And then he went on.

Little did Tommy know it, but Sarah was not asleep. She had been awake the whole time, hoping and praying that he would return safely. She had overheard some of what had transpired between Tommy and Andrew in the stairway, and she knew enough to let them work it out. And now, too, something within her told her to remain silent. She realized that Tommy was no longer a little boy and that her role in his life was changing. He would no longer need to call upon her as much as before, nor to see her as his only ally in a scary world. He was coming to trust his mom again, and the new family that welcomed him. She was both relieved and saddened that they could now depend on others.

As the sound of his footsteps faded away, she whispered, "I love you, too, little brother."

Chapter Seven
What Andrew Found

It had been such an exhausting night that everyone slept a little later than usual the next morning, which was Christmas Eve. When they gathered for breakfast, it was obvious that the crisis was over and that everyone was relieved and happy, including Tommy. Andrew brought the little bat downstairs and leaned it against his chair.

"Where did you get that, Bud?" his dad asked.

"Tommy gave it me. It's his oldest bat!" Andrew looked very proud of his new possession.

Mary was surprised, and she looked at Tommy, who just smiled and looked down at his plate. She began to understand the nature of the miracle that had taken place the night before. She knew how special the Little League bat had been to Tommy over the years. If he'd given it to Andrew, then she could only imagine what Andrew had done for him. It had to be something incredibly important.

As though he was responding to his mother's thoughts, Tommy said, "We had a little talk last night after my walk. Andrew convinced me that I belong here, too." Tommy gave Andrew a high-five, and said nothing more.

From then on, everyone was in a cheery mood, looking forward to Christmas the next day. But Andrew started to feel a little nervous as he considered the task that still lay before him. Today was the day. It was now or never: He had to buy or make his presents, whether any of them was perfect or not.

After breakfast, Andrew went into the den and sat down beside his dad, who was reading the newspaper. Stephen finally noticed that Andrew was being unusually quiet, so he asked, "Is something the matter, Bud?"

"Well, kind of. I've got to buy or make presents today. And, well, I hoped I could find something for everyone that was kind of special...you know...maybe even perfect?" He wanted desperately to tell him the whole story, and to get his help, but he was afraid that the stranger would say that Andrew had cheated. Suddenly, he remembered the boy's words again, "Don't be afraid to ask questions."

Then it dawned on him. It seemed right that he needed to figure out what to get each person, but maybe it would be okay to ask his dad to help him find or make the gifts that Andrew decided on.

"Dad, I'm making a list of the presents I want to get. Can you help me find or make them?" Andrew asked.

"Sure. Let me know when you're ready."

Andrew ran back upstairs and sat down at his desk. He reviewed the answers everyone had given him. The adults had provided answers that left him confused. And what's more, he was amazed that Sarah and Tommy had given such grown-up-like answers, too. Because he had avoided asking them what a perfect gift was, no one had said "love" or "a car," thank goodness; but the answers they gave him about what the perfect gift would do were so mind-boggling that he was afraid that he'd never be able to find anything for them.

As he concentrated on his list of questions, he began to see that the hardest puzzles sometimes have very simple solutions. In fact, he was surprised how easily ideas came to him about what to get each of the people on his list. It was as though the strange boy was standing in the corner of the room offering suggestions. Andrew even looked around to be sure the boy was not really there.

When he finished, Andrew ran back downstairs and showed his dad what he'd come up with. The expression on Stephen's face assured Andrew that he had done a good job.

"These are very creative ideas, Bud." Stephen rose from the sofa and patted Andrew on his back. "Let's go shopping!"

Two hours later, Andrew had found the presents he needed to buy, and he realized that he had three dollars and some change left. "What should I do with this extra money?" he asked his dad.

"It's up to you, Andrew, but it's supposed to be for buying presents for others," Stephen said.

As they left the store, Andrew saw a Salvation Army officer ringing a bell. So he went over and put the money into the black metal bowl. An old man in a black uniform said, "Thank you, son, and Merry Christmas!"

"Merry Christmas to you," Andrew replied. He studied the man's uniform, and asked, "Are you the commanding officer?"

"No, there's only one commanding officer," the man answered. Then he smiled and said, "I'm just one of his soldiers."

"How can I become a soldier?" Andrew asked.

"By doing what you just did," the man said.

When they got back home, Andrew laid the presents out in his room. He had been able to find something for everyone except Tommy. He just couldn't seem to locate anything at the store that would help people get along and not fight. He saw some neat boxing gloves, but he thought that might make things worse, not better. Finally, Andrew remembered something that his dad had in his office. It was a stick with feathers hanging from it, called a talking stick. His dad had told him that the Native Americans used the talking stick in their important meetings. Whenever a person held it, everyone else had to remain silent—that is, until the person handed the talking stick to someone else, who would then get a chance to talk without interruption. Andrew thought that it would be neat if Tommy and his father had a talking stick. Maybe they could listen to each other better and get along.

So, before Andrew wrapped his presents, he and his dad worked together on making Tommy's gift. They went outside and cut a stick from the hickory tree in the back yard. Then Stephen opened up his fly tying desk and took out some turkey feathers. Together they glued and tied the feathers onto the hickory stick, leaving enough time to wrap the presents before dinner.

Andrew asked everyone to stay out of his room so he and his dad could wrap the presents. The first gift that they wrapped was a picture frame and a very special photograph for his mom. A week earlier, his dad had found an old bent photo of Poppy that he had taken when he and Poppy had gone fishing several years before. Poppy was holding up a giant fish that his dad called an amberjack. After Stephen had taken the picture, they had let the fish go.

That fishing trip—15 miles off the coast of Virginia—had been one of Poppy's last adventures before he began to get sick. He looked so happy and healthy in the picture that Andrew thought it would be the perfect gift for his mom—one that would make it possible for her to keep the happy memories of Poppy alive forever. So, he flattened out the bent photo of Poppy and the fish, and he carefully inserted it in the picture frame. Then he wrapped it along with a card that said, "Mom, Now you can keep Poppy close to you forever. Love, Andrew."

The next gift he wrapped was for Cyrus. When Andrew had considered Cyrus' answer, he knew that he couldn't buy Cyrus anything that would give his stepfather more time to spend with his family. But Andrew realized that maybe he could do little things for Cyrus that would give him some time to use any way that he wanted. Andrew could fix Cyrus his daily sandwich, empty Cyrus' trash, and even clean his office. So, instead of buying Cyrus a gift at the store, Andrew decided to make Cyrus a set of coupons with which he could buy Andrew's help. He bought some colored paper and cut it up into little squares. On each piece of paper Andrew wrote down a job such as, "One Office Cleaning," or "One Trash Dumping." He prepared 10 coupons that he figured would free Cyrus from having to work for at least a couple of hours. He then wrapped them in a little box with a note that said, "Cyrus, I will do these things for you, so that you can have more time to spend with Mom. Love, Andrew."

Andrew found Gram's answer to be particularly tough at first. What could help her find something about herself that she'd lost or forgotten? As he pondered this puzzle, he recalled the doll that Gram had broken when she was a little girl. A simple solution suddenly occurred to him. He would get her a doll! A little one, of course—one that would fit inside her purse. He found one at the discount store that had blonde hair like Gram's had been when she was younger. He wrapped the little doll in tissue paper with a big pink ribbon and a card that said, "Gram, This doll is for you. Love, Andrew."

For Mary, it was difficult to figure out a way to make others feel that she was always with them. But then Andrew remembered that they sold boxes of greeting cards at the dollar store. He wrapped a box of cards along with a note that said, "Dear Mary, Now you can can reach out and touch the ones you love! Love, Andrew."

Sarah's gift was tiny, but Andrew felt really good about it. He remembered how she looked at her finger where Elliot's ring had been. Wouldn't it be nice, Andrew thought, for Sarah to have a ring just for herself? So Andrew looked in the jewelry display at the dollar store and found a ring with a big green stone in it for only $2.95. The band was adjustable, so he knew that it would always fit Sarah, no matter what. Andrew put the ring into a little box that Mary gave him. It held the ring securely on a white velvety cushion and had a lid that snapped shut. Andrew wrapped it with a card that said, "Sarah, You never have to give this one back! Love, Andrew."

Then Andrew wrapped Tommy's talking stick. His dad found a box that would keep the feathers from getting bent. Andrew wrote a little note on a card that said, "Hey Tommy, I hope this helps." He didn't want to overdo the "love" thing, so he just signed the card, "Andrew."

Finally, Andrew asked his dad to leave the room so he could wrap his present. When Andrew had thought about his dad's answer, he decided that he wanted him to feel like a winner all the time. And so, when he came upon a display of tiny trophies at the discount store, he knew that he found the very thing. He picked one out that said, "World's Greatest Dad." Andrew wrapped the tiny trophy in bright red paper and attached a little note to the base of the trophy. The note said, "Dad, You are the greatest! Love, Andrew."

Chapter Eight
What Little Beasts Need

It was dark when Andrew finished his wrapping and went downstairs with an armful of presents. He put his presents into a little pile beneath the tree where the boy had disappeared. His excitement about Christmas no longer had much to do with opening his own presents, even though he knew he'd enjoy that, too. So much had gone into his choice of presents that he couldn't wait for everyone to open them. Each gift was simple and inexpensive. And each felt like the perfect gift. But, he had no idea if the stranger would think so.

He stood before the blue ornament and looked at his own reflection in the shiny blue surface. He wondered, Would the mysterious boy come again, now that he had finished buying and making gifts for the people on his list? Would he stay and play, and come back often? What did he mean, Andrew wondered, when he said that he wouldn't have to leave if he came back? Did that mean that he was going to live at his dad's house? Obviously, there was a lot that the stranger needed to explain.

These questions and others ran through Andrew's mind, but mainly he was just happy that he'd gotten things for everybody that seemed just right for them. But one thing kept Andrew from feeling totally good. He hadn't yet gotten anything for the little beast, Diggory.

The more he thought about it, the more he knew that he would have to get the perfect monster something. But Andrew didn't feel very generous toward him. The night before, Diggory had knocked down the saloon doors in his Old West Lego town, and then he ran upstairs before Andrew could properly scold him.

He went looking for his dad to ask him for help.

Stephen was in the Christmas spirit. He was humming Christmas carols and tying fishing flies at the cherrywood desk in his bedroom. Feathers and hair covered his sweater and slacks, and they spilled over onto the rug. Somehow in the midst of it all, a buggy looking fly was getting a haircut and a pair of plastic eyes. Diggory was sleeping under the desk in the middle of the mess.

"Dad, I've got a little problem. Can you help?" Andrew asked.

"Sure, Bud," his dad replied. "What is it?" His hands were twirling around the fly like he was casting a spell.

Actually, he was finishing the fly with a special knot that would never come loose.

"I guess I need to get Diggory a present—he's the last one on my list—but he makes me so mad that it's hard to want to get him anything. If he'd only behave, it would make it easier to be nice to him."

"I know the problem. He doesn't want to learn what you want him to learn." Stephen glanced at his son, hoping that Andrew would understand that he was talking about certain little boys, too.

"Exactly! So, how can I get him a present when he's totally incorrigible?!" Andrew liked big words especially if they helped him describe something disgusting.

His dad put some glue on the fly and then turned to face Andrew. He considered how much to say to his son. After all, Andrew was only nine. But he decided to go ahead, hoping that his son would understand something that he had only really begun to grasp himself in the last few years.

"Andrew, we can teach Diggory some things, but he's always going to be a 'certain way.' He has...let's say...a nature that cannot be changed very much no matter what we do. We can teach him not to get up on the kitchen table and maybe not to rip up the toilet paper. But you know and I know that every time we wave our hands in his face, he's going to reach out and try to scratch us. It's guaranteed, without fail, right?"

"Yeah, that's for sure." Andrew agreed, frowning.

"So, when we get mad at him, it's usually because we want him to be different, and sometimes he really can't change." His dad paused to be sure Andrew was still with him. "Here's the secret as I see it..."

Andrew listened and waited.

"Everybody you love," Stephen said, "will let you down sometimes, not because they are mean or trying to upset you, but because it's their nature to be a certain way. If you want to love them, then you have to accept thatcertain things about them will probably never change."

"Does that mean I have to let Diggory in my room to make a mess of my toys?" Andrew asked, indignantly.

"No, not if you don't want to," Stephen said, thoughtfully. "Once you realize that he cannot change in some ways, you have to decide whether you need to leave the door closed or not. Loving him doesn't mean letting him do anything to you he wants to do. But loving him does mean that you don't expect him to change in ways that he can't." Stephen stopped tying and looked away, thinking of how hard this lesson had been to learn for him.

Andrew looked at one of his dad's flies that had just received a pair of bright red eyes. He thought that if he were a fish, he wouldn't eat this strange-looking fly. In fact, he'd turn and swim the other way as fast as he could. But he wasn't a fish, thank goodness. Nor a cat.

"I think I get it, Dad," Andrew said slowly. "You're saying that it will drive me crazy trying to get Diggory to change when he really can't."

"Right! And when you really accept his nature, then you really can start to love him," Stephen said.

"So, what do you think the perfect gift would do for Diggory?" Andrew asked.

His dad reached out and put his arm around him. "What you did for Tommy last night." Then he pulled Andrew closer to him, and hugged him tightly. "This," he said.

Stephen MacClean watched his son leave the room, obviously deep in thought. Even though Andrew was young, Stephen believed that his son had really understood what he had said. He hoped for Andrew's sake that he could make friends with Diggory soon, for the cat had just come down with a fever. It could be a sign that the illness was catching up with him. Diggory might not be with them much longer.

Chapter Nine
The Stranger Returns

Not knowing about Diggory's fever, Andrew went into his room and sat down on his bed. He surveyed his dinosaurs and the fenced-in compound that neatly contained his herd. He thought about the times that he had knocked them over and simply picked them up again. He thought about how much of a mess he usually made in the den and how often he forgot to take out the trash and make his bed. He liked to be neat, but he was very forgetful. Partly, he was lazy and could do better, but partly it was the way he was—it was his nature. He knew that his dad loved him the way he was, even though he kept asking Andrew to try to do better. Dad and Mary, Mom and Cyrus all seemed to know what to ask of him and what to accept about him.

As Andrew considered his own nature, he began to feel sorry for Diggory—for all of the times that he had yelled or slapped at Diggory when the cat was just being himself. He realized that he and Diggory were more alike than he'd thought. And further, he knew what the perfect gift would do for both of them. It would make them feel accepted and loved in spite of their shortcomings. Suddenly, he knew what to give the cat for Christmas. It's what Andrew himself would have wanted, and somehow he knew that it would make Diggory happier than anything else.

Andrew ran downstairs and found his markers and a piece of cardboard. Upon it he drew a picture of the blue ornament and then wrote below it in big red letters, WELCOME TO MY ROOM, DIGGORY. He wrapped the sign with some scrap pieces of Christmas paper, taped a can of Diggory's favorite wet cat food to the outside, and put it under the tree with the rest of the packages.

Christmas Eve was great fun. Dad and Mary sat by the fire listening to Christmas carols, while Tommy, Sarah, and Andrew played games on the computer, ate pizza, drank egg nog, and tried to guess what their packages contained. Andrew occasionally eyed his little pile of presents, knowing that although the gifts were simple and inexpensive, they were the very best gifts he could imagine giving to the people he loved.

Andrew decided to stay with his dad overnight, open his presents in the morning, and then go to his mom's to be with her and Cyrus and Gram. So, when it came time to go to bed, Andrew said good night and went up to his room. Sarah and Tommy followed soon afterward. For a while, Andrew just laid in his bed listening to his dad and Mary talking and laughing downstairs.

Then, everything was perfectly quiet. Andrew realized that he must have dozed off for awhile, but it seemed that only a moment had passed. He suddenly thought of Diggory, and realized that he had been missing for most of the evening. Where was he, anyway? Andrew wondered. He became worried. So, he got out of bed and walked downstairs, whispering, "Here, Diggory. Come here, boy." He went to the den and looked through the door toward the recliner, which was one of Diggory's favorite spots. But no Diggory.

"Hello, Andrew."

Andrew turned in surprise and looked toward the tree. The stranger was back! He was sitting at the foot of the Christmas tree, holding Diggory in his arms.

Andrew was stunned and simply stared at the boy. *Does this mean that I have given the perfect gift?* Andrew hoped so. Afraid that the answer might be no, though, Andrew decided to say nothing about the whole gift thing. He was afraid it would all end too soon.

"You have done well," the boy said, without explaining what he meant.

Andrew couldn't help it any longer, so he asked nervously, "Well? Did I do it? Will you stay?"

The boy smiled and nodded, "Yes, you did, and I will."

Immensely relieved and excited at the same time, Andrew went over to his little pile of gifts, and said, "Which one was it? Was it Tommy's present? I really liked that one. How about Mom's?" Andrew laid them all out at the boy's feet.

The boy put Diggory down and surveyed Andrew's collection of presents at the foot of the tree.

"Well, then, which one is it?" Andrew searched under the tree, thinking that he must have forgotten one.

"You don't understand, Andrew. Your gifts are wonderful, but they are perfect only because of something else."

Andrew gave up his search and turned to look at the boy. It was then that he saw a bluish white light shining in the middle of the boy's chest. It got brighter as Andrew stared at it. The boy then reached over and took Andrew's hand.

"Andrew, this is the perfect gift," and he lifted Andrew's hand to feel the light coming from his heart. Andrew was suddenly filled with great happiness and thankfulness. He laughed and cried and contemplated in an instant all of the things that had ever happened to him. And in that moment he couldn't think of anything that didn't seem just right.

"And, that's not all, Andrew," the boy said. "This, too, is the perfect gift." He lifted Andrew's hand to his own heart, which had begun to glow with the same wonderful brightness. Andrew's happiness grew even more, although that seemed impossible. Tears streamed down his face onto his pajamas, but he didn't even care. He was happy, incredibly happy. It was as if all the Christmas packages in all the world had been opened all at once, and everybody had received the perfect gift.

"So, does this mean that Dad was right? That love is the perfect gift?" Andrew asked, thinking back on his conversation with his dad.

"Yes," the boy said, "but it's more than that. It's what you do with your love. It's giving the very thing that someone needs the most. And that is just what you have done."

Then the boy sat down near the tree and considered Andrew's little pile of presents. He reached for the gift meant for Andrew's dad.

"Andrew, this is the perfect gift because you found a way to remind your dad that he is lovable and good. And he is." The boy put the present down beside him and picked up another one.

"And this is the perfect gift because it will let Cyrus take a break from his work, so he can spend time with those he loves. And he will." The boy then put the little package beside Stephen's present.

Andrew was speechless. The stranger knew what was in each package without having to open them!

The boy smiled, knowing what Andrew was thinking, and he went on. "Your mother's gift is perfect because it will remind her that those who have loved us never really leave us, even when they die." And then he held the wrapped-up picture of Poppy in one hand and the doll for Gram in the other. "And, Gram's gift will help her recall the most important thing that she's lost over the years." He put the two gifts down side by side.

Then the boy reached for three of the last four gifts. "Andrew, this present will help Mary stay in touch with Tommy and Sarah, no matter how far she is away from them. And, Sarah's ring will make her feel better whenever a relationship has to end. Finally, your talking stick will help Tommy remember that peace is always possible when you're willing to try."

The boy looked up at Andrew and said, "Andrew, Tommy will never forget what you did for him the other night. No matter how alone he might feel at times, he will always know that he belongs to this family, thanks to what you did."

Andrew wondered how the boy knew so much about families, so he asked, "Do you have a brother, too?"

The boy laughed, and said, "I have more brothers and sisters than you can count," knowing that Andrew would someday realize what he meant.

"Wow! Gosh...I mean...I feel sorry for your mom!" Andrew exclaimed.

Turning back to the presents that lay beneath the tree, the boy said approvingly, "You have given all of them just what they have needed."

Hearing the boy's words of approval, Andrew felt immensely relieved. But then the boy reached for the last present—the one meant for Diggory. Andrew felt a little nervousness creep back in.

"You almost forgot Diggory, didn't you?" the boy asked. Andrew looked down, feeling ashamed.

"It's okay," the boy said reassuringly. "Diggory was the most difficult test for you. But in the end, you succeeded in giving him the perfect gift, too, by inviting him into your room in spite of his annoying habits."

The boy reached out and petted the cat, who had been pawing some of the low-hanging Christmas balls. "By accepting him just the way he is, you took a step toward accepting others just the way they are, and yourself the way you are.

"Of all the perfect gifts, Andrew, that is the most precious one."

The boy then became very quiet and sat for awhile looking at the tree. Then he stood up and looked into Andrew's eyes.

"Andrew..." he said, "Because you have done what I have asked you to do, I will always be with you. Here." He touched Andrew's heart again.

Andrew didn't know what to think. And then, it finally dawned on him who the stranger was.

"You can make Diggory well, can't you? Would you? Please?" Andrew picked Diggory up and held the cat between himself and the boy, hoping that the boy would do something to take Diggory's illness away.

The boy rubbed Diggory's ears, and the cat purred happily. "Maybe I could. But your love can do amazing things, too. And anyway, death isn't half as bad as you think. It's just a different kind of living."

The boy stepped aside to reveal the bright blue ball.

"Welcome to my room, Andrew," the boy said.

As Andrew looked into the blue ornament, he saw many things. He saw a bearded man in a robe with his arms full of flowers, and then a beautiful lady who smiled at him with the most tender, loving expression. Then he saw someone he knew. Andrew exclaimed, "It's a picture of Poppy!" But then, as he looked again, the man smiled at him.

"Hi, kid."

"Poppy, you're alive!" Andrew exclaimed as he gazed tearfully into the bright blue ornament. "I love you, Poppy!"

"I love you too, kid. I'm glad you can see me, because I'm here all the time."

As Andrew looked blissfully at his Poppy's smiling face, the light began to get brighter and brighter. Poppy would soon be invisible again.

Looking back, Andrew saw that the boy, too, was fading into the light. "But you promised that you would stay with me," Andrew said.

"As long as you give the perfect gift," the boy said, "I will be as close to you as your own heart." Then the boy began to blend with the light of the ornament.

"Please don't leave," Andrew pleaded.

The boy said, "Andrew, Don't be afraid—I will always be with you."

Andrew nodded tearfully. "Okay," he said, as he watched the boy and Poppy fade into the light.

Then everything became ordinary again. He stood for a moment and looked around the room. "This was no dream," Andrew said to Diggory.

Diggory rubbed against Andrew's leg. Andrew bent down and picked him up with his present, and carried them to his room. He put the feverish cat next to his pillow, and put the package next to the cat so he would see it first thing on Christmas morning. He rubbed Diggory's neck and ears until he was purring and drifting off to sleep.

"Welcome to my room, Diggory," Andrew whispered.

www.ingramcontent.com/pod-product-compliance
Lightning Source LLC
Chambersburg PA
CBHW070610310726
48982CB00001B/31

* 9 7 8 0 9 6 6 5 4 8 5 6 3 *